THE CHRISTMAS ROSE

Sepp Bauer

Illustrated by **Else Wenz-Viëtor**

🌉 Charlesbridge

2008 First U.S. edition
Translation copyright © 2008 by Charlesbridge Publishing
Translated by Ben W. L. Sachtler

Published by Charlesbridge
85 Main Street
Watertown, MA 02472
(617) 926-0329
www.charlesbridge.com

First published in Germany under the title *Die Christrose*
Copyright © 2006 by Lappan Verlag GmbH, D-26121 Oldenburg, Germany

Library of Congress Cataloging-in-Publication Data is available upon request.

Printed in China
(hc) 10 9 8 7 6 5 4 3 2 1

Display type and text type set in New Century Schoolbook
Printed and bound by Toppan Printing Company
Production supervision by Brian G. Walker
Designed by Martha MacLeod Sikkema

CHRISTMAS IN GERMANY

Saint Nikolaus was a fourth-century bishop who is said to have given gifts to the poor and helped prevent injustice. In the German tradition Saint Nikolaus brings small gifts, such as apples, chocolate, and gingerbread, to children on December 6. The presents are placed in the children's shoes, which are left out the night before. Saint Nikolaus is often accompanied by his servant, Knecht Ruprecht, who carries a rod to punish naughty children. The roles of judge and benefactor are sometimes combined in Saint Nikolaus, and this dual nature is reflected in today's Santa Claus.

Germans celebrate Christmas on the evening of December 24. In many parts of Germany, especially the South, presents are brought by an angel known as the Christ Child. The historical origin of the Christ Child may lie in early Christmas pageants. Young participants, called Christ children, dressed as angels and brought gifts to the infant Jesus. In modern pageants, the part of the Christ Child is often played by a girl. The Christ Child is usually depicted as a blond angel wearing a gold crown and angelic robes and is not necessarily the baby Jesus himself.

"**L**ook—a falling star!" the poor woodsman exclaimed, raising himself in bed and gazing out the window at the sparkling heavens. He sank back onto his pillow and sighed, his cheeks pale and hollow. He was very, very ill. He feebly patted the hands of his children, Fritz and Gretl, who sat at his bedside.

"Every day I get worse," the woodsman said. "I fear I will never be well again, and then what shall become of you and your mother?"

Fritz said, "Father, you *will* be well again. I will ask Saint Nikolaus about a cure for your illness when he comes today. Surely he will know. You must get well!" The woodsman smiled sadly and closed his tired eyes.

The children waited anxiously by the door for Saint Nikolaus's arrival. At last they saw a figure approaching on the path.

"I think it is him," whispered Gretl. Fritz opened the door and ran outside.

"Dear Saint Nikolaus," said Fritz, "surely you know that our father is very ill. Please, please, tell us how we can help him."

"Well, my boy," said Saint Nikolaus, "you and your little sister can indeed help your father, but it will be difficult, terribly difficult. Listen carefully. Far up in the North lives the Winter King. He grows white winter roses in his fortress. If you bring home one of these flowers, your father will be saved, because anyone who breathes the flower's scent is cured of all illness. The journey to the Winter Land is long and dangerous, however. Very rarely does anyone succeed. Are you and Gretl prepared to undertake such a journey?"

Fritz nodded.

"That is very brave of you, for you will have to bear many hardships. Here, let me give you this key. It will serve you in a time of dire need. I cannot say more than that." Saint Nikolaus went inside the house to the poor woodsman's bedside and wished him a swift recovery. Then he opened his big bag, gave the children many wonderful presents, and left.

Early the next morning, while Fritz and Gretl's parents were still asleep, Fritz wrote them a note:

> *Dear Mama and Papa,*
> *We are going to see the Winter King to get a miracle flower that will make Papa well again. Saint Nikolaus said it will work. Don't worry about us.*
> *A thousand kisses,*
> *Fritz and Gretl*

The children filled a backpack with all the gifts that Saint Nikolaus had given them, put the letter on the kitchen table, and left.

"Which way is it to the Winter King?" asked Gretl.

"I don't know," answered Fritz, "but we will find out." Deep snow covered the forest that surrounded them. Which way should they go?

"We could ask the squirrel," Fritz suggested. "He knows the forest very well." Standing under a tall beech tree, he called, "Mister Squirrel, Mister Squirrel, come on out!" The little creature popped out of his nest.

"What do you want?"

"Please, dear squirrel, can you show us how to get to the Winter King?"

"I do not know the way. You had better ask Crookshanks, the hare. He is ancient and knows everything."

After the squirrel had slipped back into his nest, Fritz and Gretl went to see the old hare Crookshanks. He was sitting under a bushy fir tree. He looked at the two children with wise eyes and listened attentively as Fritz told him the reason for their visit.

The hare thought awhile, scratched behind his long ears, and looked very serious.

"Well," he said finally, "it is good of you to want to help your sick father, but . . ." He shook his head, muttering. "You will have to endure a lot, I can tell you that. It is a very, very long way to the Winter King."

Then he looked into the children's pleading eyes. After a moment he said, "Come with me. I will take you to the deer. She runs as fast as the wind and may be able to help you." Off he hopped, his tail bobbing up and down.

Fritz was joyful. He nudged Gretl, saying, "See, it is not impossible. Just wait, we will get help for Papa." The two children ran through the forest after the hare.

Crookshanks explained to the deer who Fritz and Gretl were and why they were there. The deer looked at the two children with such kindness and friendliness that they stepped closer to pet her smooth fur.

"Climb onto my back," said the deer. "I will carry you as far as I can."

"Won't we be too heavy? Can you really carry both of us?" Gretl asked.

"I am strong," replied the animal. The children climbed onto her back and held on. Crookshanks waved goodbye with his ears and called after them, "Good luck!"

The deer began to run, and the wind whistled past them. Hour after hour the deer ran through the forest, over fields, and across the open heath, until they came to a vast, snow-covered plain.

The deer stopped there and bade the children to dismount. "This is the edge of my territory, so I cannot carry you farther," she said. "Now the reindeer must help you. We are good friends, and I am sure he will help if I ask him."

When the reindeer heard from the deer where the children wanted to go, he exclaimed, "Oh, children, turn back while you still can! It is a terribly long way to the Winter King. You could easily freeze to death in the icy wasteland that lies ahead."

Gretl said, "We must see the Winter King! Our dear papa has to get well again. We will endure it all without complaint, we promise."

The reindeer looked at the children for a long time. Finally he said, "Climb onto my back."

Fritz and Gretl thanked the deer for having brought them this far, and—whoosh!—the reindeer took off. Blasts of white, steamy breath shot from his mouth, and his hooves kicked up clouds of snow. With huge bounds the powerful animal stormed northward.

Fritz held on to the stout neck of the reindeer with both hands, and Gretl wrapped her cold arms around her brother. They raced across the snow-covered land for a long, long time.

"The sea!" announced the reindeer at last, stopping at the shore. Steam rose from his mouth. Fritz climbed off the reindeer's back and helped Gretl down. The ocean stretched endlessly before them. How would they cross it?

"It's all over now, Fritz," Gretl cried sadly, rubbing her icy hands.

"We must find a way across the sea," Fritz said. "Who can help us?"

The reindeer gave three long, bellowing calls. His voice echoed over the water. There was a rush of air, and an enormous bird swooped toward them.

"The wild goose here will carry you over the sea to the icebergs," said the reindeer.

"Will that be the end of our journey?" asked Fritz.

"No, my boy. I warned you—it is still a long way to the Winter King. Safe journey, brave children!"

The wild goose gave a loud honk when they sat on her back, and then rose into the air. Quick as an arrow she flew north over the sea. Gretl pressed herself against Fritz and hardly dared to look down from the dizzying height.

Fritz could barely hold on to the wild goose with his shivering hands, but he knew that he must not let go. If he did, he and Gretl would fall into the depths of the sea. Fritz stared straight ahead without blinking. Tears ran from his eyes and froze to ice on his cheeks. Gretl had fallen asleep behind him, having tied herself to him with a scarf. How much longer would they have to fly like this?

At last Fritz saw icebergs glittering in the distance. The goose gave a loud honk and steered toward them. Soon the goose landed and let the children off her back. It was frightfully cold. As the children looked around, the wild goose squawked once more and flew away. Had she abandoned them?

The children were huddled together to keep warm when a polar bear lumbered toward them, called by the goose's squawk. Fritz quickly reached into his backpack and held out an apple, one of the gifts from Saint Nikolaus. The polar bear ate the apple, gave a satisfied grunt, and lay down on the ground so the children could easily climb onto his back. Then—whoosh!—he strode off across the ice with mighty steps.

The children rode ever farther north on the polar bear's back. The wind whipped heavy snowflakes into their faces. How that hurt!

Fritz felt Gretl sobbing behind him. He patted her hands, saying, "Dear little sister, think of our papa with all your might and be brave. We must bring him the white rose. We must!"

Gretl clung more tightly to her brother and was quiet. A thick fog began to wrap around them, and soon it was impossible to see. Suddenly a mighty voice thundered, "STOP!" Fritz was so startled that he nearly fell off the polar bear.

A snow giant, bigger than a tree, stepped out from behind an icy mountain and asked, "Where are you going, you puny little humans?"

"We want to see the Winter King," said Fritz, thinking quickly. "Here is a gift from Saint Nikolaus. Can you help us, please?" He reached into the backpack and pulled out the largest gingerbread man he had. The children climbed off the polar bear's back, and Fritz handed the gingerbread man to the giant.

"Well, well," said the amused giant, giving a friendly grin. "Come along then!"

The giant placed Fritz and Gretl into his pocket and strode off. While the air got colder and colder outside, the children were warm and cozy. How long were they carried in the giant's pocket? They did not know.

At last the snow giant lifted them out, saying, "We have arrived, humanlings. There is the Winter King's fortress." He put the children down in the snow and headed back the way he had come.

Fritz and Gretl stood before a gloomy fortress covered in snow and ice. As they stepped inside, a terrible chill crept into their hearts. The two children walked hesitantly down a dark passageway and arrived in a great hall.

The Winter King sat there on a throne of ice. A huge, white beard flowed onto his chest, and a heavy royal robe hung over his shoulders. He sat perfectly still, but green lightning bolts flashed in his eyes like distant thunderstorms. Two polar bears rested at his feet, their heads on their paws, staring straight at the children.

Fritz and Gretl stood frozen with fear in the great hall of the fortress.

"Who are you, and what do you want?" asked the Winter King in a rumbling voice. His breath shot over them like an icy north wind. Fritz and Gretl trembled and could not say a word. Then Fritz thought of the loving, tired eyes of his father and drew up his courage.

"Winter King," he said, "my name is Fritz, and this is my sister, Gretl. We beg you with all our hearts to give us one of your white winter roses. Our father is ill and can only be cured by your flower. Please help us."

Gretl took a step forward, held out her hands, and cried out in a voice choked with tears, "Please . . . please!" She was unable to say anything more.

The Winter King remained motionless. Then he nodded and ordered, "Bring a flower!"

A little mouse soon scurried in, carrying a winter rose. On the slender stem hung an unscented white bud. The flower had not yet bloomed.

he Winter King could see that the children were disappointed with the flower.

"Listen, children. The bud will open only when the Christ Child blesses it. You must go see the Christ Child now, or the bud will do you no good." He whistled, and two white wolves slunk into the hall. They stared at the children with glowing eyes, growled angrily, and bared their sharp fangs.

"Go prepare the carriage!" the Winter King ordered the wolves. "Take the children safely to the wall of heaven. Woe to you if anything happens to them!"

The wolves howled, ran out of the hall, and returned with the Winter King's carriage.

"Take the flower bud and get in," said the Winter King to Fritz and Gretl. Before they could thank him, he ordered, "Begone!" The wolves pulled the carriage, and it shot out of the fortress into the icy wasteland.

"How grim he is," said Gretl.

"It doesn't matter," crowed Fritz jubilantly. "We have the miracle flower!"

The wolves raced all through the night. At dawn the carriage arrived at a great wall that reached into the clouds above.

The wolves growled, and Fritz and Gretl got out of the carriage. In fear and awe the children stared up at the wall that towered forbiddingly above them. The wolves pulled the carriage around and ran off, leaving the children all alone.

"This is the wall of heaven," Fritz whispered. "We must get inside—we must. Come on, let us find a gate."

The children searched and searched, but they could find no path or tracks in the snow that might lead them to a gate. The wind roared against the massive wall, ripping the clouds to shreds as it dragged them over the top of the gloomy towers. Every now and then, though, during a lull, what sounded like a sweet chorus of voices and tinkling bells drifted over from the other side.

The children shouted, but their voices were lost in the vast, desolate space. They fought desperately through the snow to find an entrance, but their efforts were in vain.

"Are we to die so near our goal?" asked Gretl wretchedly. "That must not be!"

"Sit down, Gretl, and rest," said Fritz. "I will keep searching." He went off again, and at last as he turned a corner he saw a small hidden door. He called out quickly, "I found a door, Gretl! Over here!"

They turned the rusty handle, but the door was locked. They rattled the door, shouting and hammering against the wood with their small fists. Nothing happened. The door stayed shut.

At this latest disappointment the usually hopeful Fritz began to cry. Weeping, he sat down in the snow. "It is over— all is lost!" he sobbed. "Everything was for naught." Gretl stroked his hair and tried to comfort him. Then she had a sudden thought.

"Fritz! Why don't we try the key that Saint Nikolaus gave us?" she asked.

"Ah—the key! Yes, the key!" Fritz jumped up, wiped the tears from his face, and exclaimed, "How could I have forgotten the key?"

He pulled the key from the backpack. Trembling with excitement, he put it in the lock and—creak!—the door sprang open.

As Fritz and Gretl walked through the heavenly gate, they were bathed in radiant, streaming light. What a glorious world! A warm wind caressed their cheeks. Sun-drenched meadows covered in flowers greeted them, and a blue sky stretched overhead. What joy and delight!

The children stood and stared, their brave hearts rejoicing. The ice melted off their clothes, and all exhaustion and pain fell away from them.

As they looked on blissfully, a small angel flew toward them and asked kindly, "Who are you? Where do you come from, dear children?"

Fritz and Gretl told him everything. The little angel exclaimed, "Oh, I am so happy that you made it safely through that terribly long journey. To think of all you went through! Isn't it wonderful that you are finally with us? Come, let us go see Uncle Nikolaus."

"Saint Nikolaus?" the children marveled. "Does he live here, too?"

The little angel led them through a meadow. Suddenly Gretl stopped and pulled on Fritz's sleeve.

"Look over there, Fritz," she whispered. Behind a cloud sat a group of little angels working busily.

"Oh, how beautiful," said Gretl. "I am sure they are preparing for Christmas."

"Go on and take a look," said their guide.

"But surely we are not allowed to do that?" asked Fritz. "At home we are not allowed to watch when the angels decorate the Christmas tree and bring the presents."

"Here you may see everything!" the little angels called out cheerfully, waving them to come closer. There was so much to see! Nuts, apples, gingerbread, chocolate, and other delicious treats were piled into mountains.

Thousands of dolls and teddy bears waited to be wrapped as gifts. The little angels busily hammered and sawed, sanded and glued, kneaded dough and baked. The children watched them in delight.

Fritz and Gretl stood there for a long time. Their cheeks were flushed and their eyes glowed. They could not get enough of the bustling little angels. It was all so wonderful to see!

"We really should go see Uncle Nikolaus," said their companion at last. "Come!"

The children said goodbye to the other little angels and followed their guide to Saint Nikolaus's house.

"God bless you, dear children!" Saint Nikolaus cried, rushing out to meet them. "You have been very brave. I am so happy to see you again!"

Fritz and Gretl told him all about their journey. Then Fritz reached into his pocket and pulled out the key. "Thank you for the key, Saint Nikolaus," he said. "It was a great help to us. Maybe it can help other children now."

Saint Nikolaus smiled and patted their cheeks. In a kind, gentle voice he said, "Come, let us visit the Christ Child."

The children's eyes widened. Gretl whispered, "Visit . . . the Christ Child?"

ritz, Gretl, and Saint Nikolaus had not walked far when they heard jingling bells in the distance. A carriage pulled by white deer came toward them.

"Ah, children, we are in luck," said Saint Nikolaus. "Here comes the Christ Child."

"The Christ Child!" The children hardly dared to breathe. The carriage stopped before them, and the Christ Child stepped out. Oh, how beautiful the Christ Child was! How joyfully its eyes twinkled! How sweet its voice rang! Fritz and Gretl knelt by the side of the road and did not dare to look up.

Saint Nikolaus explained the reason for Fritz and Gretl's long journey. The Christ Child listened attentively. Then it approached the children and gave them each a loving kiss. The Christ Child blessed the bud that the Winter King had given them. Behold! The bud opened and a wonderful scent streamed from the flower.

"A Christmas rose," whispered Fritz, filled with great joy.

"Tomorrow evening I descend to earth," announced the Christ Child, "and you will come with me."

That night Fritz and Gretl were so excited that they did not sleep a wink. They rested during the next day, and in the evening a little angel came to bring them to the Christ Child's carriage. Saint Nikolaus was the coachman, and the Christ Child sat beside him.

A dazzlingly beautiful Christmas tree covered with blazing candles stood in the carriage. Behind it was room for Fritz and Gretl to sit. All around the carriage flew little angels with small Christmas trees in their hands. The heavens filled with angelic laughter and blissful joy.

Saint Nikolaus smiled as the carriage gently floated through the starry night. What a radiant, festive procession! Slowly the heavenly travelers drifted down toward earth. Soon they could hear bells ringing and human voices raised in a jubilant chorus.

When they arrived on earth, the Christ Child said, "You may get out now, children. Merry Christmas!"

Saint Nikolaus shook hands with them, and the Christ Child waved at them one last time. Fritz and Gretl watched the heavenly carriage disappear behind the trees. Silence and darkness fell around them, but then the Christmas rose began to shine brightly in their hands. The two children recognized the path on which they were standing.

"It is the path to our house!" Gretl cried joyfully, and soon they saw a Christmas tree glowing through a familiar window. Fritz and Gretl's mother rushed out to greet them. Embracing them, all she could say was, "My dear, dear children."

Fritz and Gretl ran toward the house, calling, "Papa, Papa, we brought you the Christmas rose!" No sooner had their father inhaled the scent of the white flower than the color returned to his cheeks and his tired eyes glowed with new life. He jumped up, completely cured, and held his brave children against his heart.

No one ever had a more joyful Christmas than the poor woodsman and his family!

ABOUT THE BOOK

The Christmas Rose was first published around 1920 as a kind of advent calendar. The stories and pictures for two days appeared on each page. Each picture was printed in color on white paper, cut out, and glued down on cardboard that had been printed with the text. After its original publication, the book went out of print and was all but forgotten.

A German editor learned about the existence of *The Christmas Rose* from one of Wenz-Viëtor's daughters. Although the daughter remembered the book, she did not have a copy of it. The original illustrations were also gone, probably destroyed during World War II.

Luckily, after searching through many used bookstores, the editor was able to purchase a copy of the original book from an antiquarian bookseller in Switzerland in 2006. *The Christmas Rose* was soon reissued in Germany as a thirty-two-page picture book, with one day on each page. In this forty-eight-page American edition, the book is smaller and upright, with one day on each two-page spread.

Just as Christmas traditions evolve, *The Christmas Rose* has been altered by its journey through time and across cultures. This lost treasure, rediscovered for a new generation, reminds us of the enduring strength of the Christmas spirit.